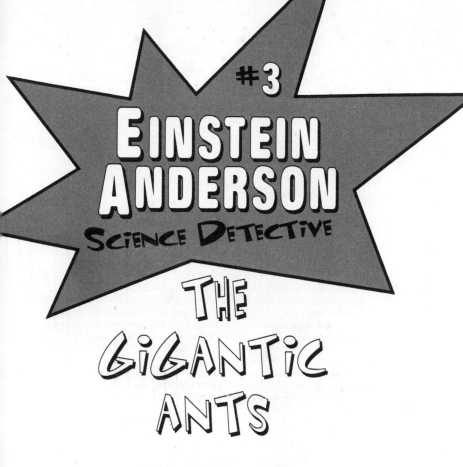

#3

# EINSTEIN ANDERSON

## SCIENCE DETECTIVE

# THE GIGANTIC ANTS

## AND OTHER CASES

by Seymour Simon

illustrated by S. D. Schindler

**Morrow Junior Books**
**NEW YORK**

(Previously published as *Einstein Anderson Makes Up for Lost Time*)

*For my wife,*
*Joyce Shanock Simon,*
*with my love*

Text copyright © 1981, 1997 by Seymour Simon
Illustrations copyright © 1997 by S. D. Schindler

First published in 1981 by Viking Penguin
under the title *Einstein Anderson Makes Up for Lost Time.*
Revised hardcover edition published by Morrow Junior Books in 1997.
Published by arrangement with the author.

Printed in the United States of America.

1  2  3  4  5  6  7  8  9  10

Library of Congress Cataloging-in-Publication Data
Simon, Seymour.
The gigantic ants and other cases/by Seymour Simon;
illustrated by S. D. Schindler.—Rev. ed.
p. cm.—(Einstein Anderson, science detective)
Rev. ed. of: *Einstein Anderson makes up for lost time.* 1986, © 1981.
Summary: Einstein Anderson uses his scientific knowledge
to solve a variety of puzzles, including a snake that
chases people and a machine that can stop hurricanes.
ISBN 0-688-14439-X
[1. Science—Problems, exercises, etc.—Fiction.]   I. Schindler, S. D., ill.
II. Simon, Seymour. Einstein Anderson makes up for lost time.   III. Title.
IV. Series: Simon, Seymour. Einstein Anderson, science detective.
PZ7.S60573Gi 1997   [Fic]—dc20   96-41767   CIP AC

# CONTENTS

# 1

## The Case of the

# SPEEDY SNAKE

instein Anderson awoke one Saturday morning in April to the sound of a loud crash. There were a few seconds of silence, then Einstein heard another loud crash. The noise was coming from the next-door bedroom of his younger brother, Dennis.

Einstein rubbed his eyes and stretched. What was going on? Had he overslept? That couldn't be right, he decided. He knew that sunrise was about 5:30 A.M. this week, and the sky was just now getting light outside his window.

"Dennis, are you making that racket?" Einstein called out. "Don't you know it's Saturday and there's no school? Why are you up so early?"

"Who's that?" Dennis asked innocently, as if he didn't know. "Is that you, Einstein? Did I wake you up? I'm *so* sorry. I'm thinking of going fishing this morning, and I...accidentally...dropped my boots on the floor."

"Your *boots*?" grumbled Einstein. "They sounded like a horse taking tap-dancing lessons."

"Ha, ha. That's really funny, Einstein," Dennis said, coming into his brother's room. "Say, as long as you're up, how would you like to go fishing with me? Mom said she didn't want me going by myself but that I could go if you'd go. Will you go, please?"

So that was why Dennis had dropped the boots, "accidentally." Einstein sighed and pulled the covers over his head. He wondered how Dennis had managed to wake up so early. Dennis didn't have an alarm clock. He usually didn't need one. Einstein was always more than happy to wake up Dennis on school days. I suppose it's only fair for me to take Dennis fishing, Einstein decided.

"O.K., let's go," he said. "I'll get dressed. Then we can have a light breakfast and pack a few peanut butter and jelly sandwiches and some fruit in case we get hungry. You make the sandwiches and I'll make breakfast."

Einstein dressed rapidly and went down to the kitchen. He poured two glasses of orange juice, filled two bowls with cereal and milk, and popped some slices of bread into the toaster. The boys had almost finished eating when their father walked into the kitchen.

"I'm surprised to see you boys up so early," said Dr. Anderson. He was a veterinarian and often went out to see a sick animal even before his sons got up in the morning.

"Is that all you're eating for breakfast, Adam?" Dr. Anderson said with affection. "No pancakes, French toast, or eggs?"

"Talking about eggs reminds me of something, Dad," Einstein said. "Did you hear that Mr. Norton's hens stopped laying eggs?"

"No, he didn't tell me that. I'd better stop over at his farm."

"Don't bother," said Einstein. "His hens are just tired of working for chicken feed."

Dr. Anderson groaned. "Adam," he said, "your jokes are worse than ever."

Adam was Einstein's real name. But almost everyone called him Einstein, after the most famous scientist of the twentieth century. Adam had been interested in science for as long as he could remember. He talked about science, read about science, experimented in science, and even solved puzzles by using science. For years even his teachers had called him by the nickname of Einstein.

Einstein Anderson was an average-size twelve-year-old boy in the sixth grade. Sometimes his light brown eyes had a faraway look when he was thinking about some important problem in science. But Einstein was not always serious. He loved jokes of all kinds and liked to make puns, the worse the better.

After Einstein and Dennis finished breakfast, they stacked the dishes in the sink. They promised their father they would wash them when they got home from fishing. Then they took their fishing equipment and the sandwiches and left the house.

The sun had come up while the boys were having breakfast. It was a bright day but very chilly. They stowed their gear on their bikes and started off to Potter's Pond.

Along the way they stopped to rest. Dennis found a snake's skin beneath some bushes and showed it to his brother.

"How did this happen?" Dennis asked. "Did the snake die and leave its skin?"

"No," answered Einstein. "A living snake sheds its skin from time to time. A new skin will form under the old one. Then the old skin breaks, and the snake begins to crawl out of it. The old skin is turned inside out, usually in one filmy piece like this one. You can see the snake's scales reproduced in the skin." He put the skin into the bike bag to look at later.

"Gee," Dennis said, "I wonder how a snake feels when it sheds its skin."

"It feels *snaked,*" said Einstein.

"Sorry I asked," Dennis said as he got back on his bike.

At the pond they leaned their bikes against a nearby tree. They took their poles and the box of fishing equipment and set off for their favorite spot—a large rock at the pond's edge.

There they contentedly fished for an hour or two. The only thing Dennis caught was a small yellow perch. He decided to let it go because it was not particularly good for eating and was too small besides. Once Einstein had a smallmouth bass on his line, but it got away. Like all fishermen, he claimed it was at least a foot long. But Dennis said it looked like no more than three inches to him.

The boys got hungry after a while and decided to eat the sandwiches they had brought. They were just about to pack up and start back to their bikes when they saw someone running toward them.

Einstein pushed back his glasses and looked at the figure coming nearer. "Oh, no," he said. "It's Pat Burns. I wonder what that pest is up to."

Pat Burns was the biggest kid in Einstein's class. He was also the meanest. Most of the other kids called him Pat the Brat, but not to his face. He was too big.

"Hello, Pat," Einstein said when his classmate got closer. "Who are you running from?"

"Do you see a snake still chasing me?" said Pat, out of breath. He stopped and looked around. "Whew, that was a close call. I guess the snake must have gone for your sandwiches when I threw them at him. Well, at least he didn't bite me. And after all, a couple of peanut butter and jelly sandwiches are worth not getting bitten, right?"

"Peanut butter and jelly sandwiches! You mean *our* sandwiches? You took our sandwiches and gave them to a snake?"

"I didn't *want* to give the sandwiches to the snake, Einstein," Pat said innocently. "I saw you two fishing down here, and I thought you might be getting hungry. So I took the sandwiches out of the bags on your bikes. I was bringing them down to you when this snake came along and tried to bite me. I started running, but the snake followed me and was even catching up. So I threw the sandwiches at him to distract him, and I got away."

"That is one of the silliest stories I have ever heard," Einstein said. "You probably ate our sandwiches and then just made up that story to try to fool us."

"You can't prove that," said Pat, beginning to look mad. "I've seen snakes around here plenty of times. I even saw that you have a snake's skin in your bike bag. So how do you know my story isn't true?"

*Can you solve the mystery:* How did Einstein
know that Pat was not telling the truth?

"Your story is impossible," Einstein said.

"Why? Snakes chase people, don't they?"

"That might be true," Einstein said. "But it would be very unlikely. Snakes go after frogs, fish, insects, and other small animals. But most snakes will just get out of the way if a person comes too close. They'll hiss and even bite if they're cornered, but they're hardly likely to chase a person."

"Well, this one did," said Pat.

"And you said he was catching up to you?" asked Einstein.

"That's right," Pat said. "I was running as fast as I could, and that snake was getting closer and closer. So I just dropped the sandwiches, hoping the snake would go for them instead of me."

"Sorry, Pat, but that's just wrong," said Einstein. "No snake can catch a running person. The fastest snake in the world, the black mamba that lives in Africa, can move only about four or five miles an hour. You can easily run faster than that. A good sprinter can run faster than twenty miles an hour."

Pat laughed and slapped Einstein on the

back. "It was all just a joke," he said. "And anyway, I knew you'd enjoy the story about the snake. I had a real brainstorm went I thought it up."

"Some brainstorm," Einstein said as he and Dennis turned to walk back to their bikes. "It seemed more like a light drizzle to me. The next time you get a bright idea it will be beginner's luck."

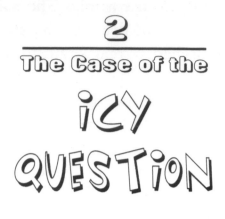

# 2

## The Case of the

# iCY QUESTiON

t was Saturday, a week after Einstein had been awakened by Dennis to go fishing. Einstein had wanted to sleep late, but he had promised his friend Margaret Michaels that he would come over early to do some science experiments in the morning. Then they would eat lunch and go over to the school yard to play softball.

Margaret was Einstein's friend and classmate. She was about as tall as Einstein and good at sports. Science was her favorite subject, too. Einstein and Margaret were always working with microscopes, telescopes, and other scientific instruments. They enjoyed talking to each other about such important subjects as solar energy, ecology, astronomy, and who was the best science student at Sparta Middle School.

When Einstein arrived at Margaret's house, she was just feeding her tropical fish. There were several different kinds. They were all at the surface of the water, grabbing for the food with wide-open mouths.

Einstein looked at the fish for a minute and then turned to Margaret. "Do you know what one fish said to the other?" he said.

Margaret knew Einstein liked bad jokes. "What?" she said suspiciously.

"If you keep your big mouth shut, you won't get caught."

"I shouldn't have asked," Margaret said, shaking back her red hair. "I've got to feed Orville and Wilbur and take Nova for a walk, and then we can do some science experiments." Orville and Wilbur were Margaret's two cats, and Nova was her dog. Margaret hadn't named her tropical fish yet.

13

After Margaret and Einstein had taken care of her pets, they went into the kitchen. The table had been cleared of dishes, and on it were a knife, some wire, a chemical scale with brass weights, and an alcohol burner.

"I thought we'd do experiments with ice and physical changes," said Margaret.

She opened the refrigerator and took out a large block of ice from the freezer compartment. She placed the ice block on top of a plastic dish rack in the sink.

"Einstein," she said, "can you cut through this chunk of ice and still leave one solid block of ice behind?"

"What?" Einstein asked. "How can you cut through ice and not get more than one piece?"

"That's for me to know and you to find out," said Margaret. "Here's a hint. I hope you don't feel too much pressure in solving the puzzle."

Einstein went over to the ice. "If I heat the knife or a piece of the wire, it will cut through the ice," he said, thinking out loud.

"But then you'll have two pieces of ice left," said Margaret. "Do you give up?"

"Just a minute," Einstein said. He pushed back his glasses and was quiet. Then his face lit up. "If you give me a piece of wire and two bricks," he said, "I'll do it."

*Can you solve the mystery:* How can Einstein cut through a block of ice and yet leave a solid block behind?

15

Margaret's face fell. She rubbed her freckled nose. "As soon as you asked for two bricks, I knew you could do it," she said. "Can you use these two brass weights instead of the bricks?" she asked.

"Sure," said Einstein. "Let's work on it together."

Einstein and Margaret tied a brass weight to each end of a piece of thin wire. Then they placed the weighted wire on top of the ice. Slowly the wire began to pass through the ice, yet it left a solid block behind.

"Your clue was a good one, Margaret," Einstein explained. "You said something about pressure. And pressure is the key to the puzzle. The ice directly under the wire melts because the pressure of the wire lowers the melting point of the ice. The ice changes to water, and the wire slips down. But the water freezes again as the wire passes through and the pressure is released."

"You're right as usual," said Margaret. "Ice melting under pressure is really the principle that explains ice-skating. The ice melts beneath the weight of the skates, and the skates move easily."

"I guess you could say that melting ice is just skid stuff," said Einstein.

"I could," Margaret said, "but I'd rather not."

# 3

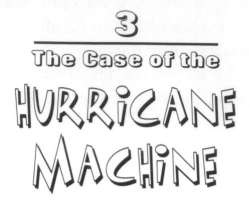

## The Case of the HURRICANE MACHINE

**A**dam, do you think a person could invent a machine that's able to stop a hurricane in its tracks?" Mrs. Anderson asked her son one morning at breakfast.

Mrs. Anderson worked as a writer and editor on the Sparta *Tribune,* one of the town's two newspapers. She often asked Einstein to check on the scientific accuracy of stories she wrote for the paper.

"I haven't read anything about a machine

like that in *Scientific American* or any of the other science magazines recently," her son answered. "Why do you ask?"

"I'm supposed to write an article about a Professor Rayn who's coming to town to give a lecture tonight in the school auditorium. He claims he's a scientist working on a machine that will stop hurricanes. Rayn is going from town to town, raising funds so he can continue his research. I'd like you to come with me to hear the lecture and then tell me what you think."

"Well, I can tell you one thing about hurricanes," Einstein said. "They used to be named only after females, but now they're named after both males and females."

"That's certainly reasonable," Mrs. Anderson said.

"Yes," Einstein continued, "except that some people think the hurricanes named after males should be called himmicanes."

Mrs. Anderson groaned. "I'll overlook that terrible joke," she said, "if you'll come with me this evening to hear the lecture."

"Be glad to, Mom," said Einstein.

That evening the school auditorium was crowded with people. Mrs. Anderson and Einstein had arrived early and found seats in the front. Mrs. Anderson was ready with a pencil and a notebook.

When Professor Rayn came out on the stage, the audience applauded politely. He had a beard and was dressed in a white lab coat. He introduced himself, and then, after a short general discussion about hurricanes, he began to talk about why he had come to Sparta.

"Ladies and gentlemen," he said, "my hurricane stopper is a most marvelous machine. It can stop a hurricane in its tracks. I need just a few thousand dollars more to complete my work on the machine. And I hope to raise that money here in Sparta. I know you will all help me reach that goal so that I can save human life and property."

"That certainly sounds worthwhile, Adam," whispered Mrs. Anderson. "What do you think so far?"

"Oh, there's no doubt that a machine that can stop a hurricane would be an important scientific advance," Einstein whispered back. "But the professor hasn't said anything about how his machine works. Suppose I ask him."

"Go ahead, Einstein. But be sure to be polite."

Einstein raised his hand. The professor said, "Yes, young man? What can I do for you?"

"I wonder if you can tell us something about how your machine works?" asked Einstein.

"Well, I'm afraid that would be much too difficult for you to understand. But I will give you some more facts about hurricanes, and then I will tell you simply how my machine can stop one from blowing.

"Hurricanes are storms with winds that blow very hard, more than seventy-five miles an hour. A large hurricane might be hundreds of miles across. A hurricane can flatten houses, blow down trees, and pick up cars and hurl them through the air. My machine will prevent the hurricane from forming by giving off electrical particles into the air. Does that answer your question, young man? Good. Now let's get back to my machine and the help I need to complete—"

"Excuse me, Professor," said Ms. Taylor, Einstein's sixth-grade science teacher, who was sitting in the audience, "but could you explain how your machine is going to stop a hurricane with electrical particles?"

Professor Rayn obviously didn't like the question. "A hurricane," he said quickly, "is an extreme high-pressure area. The high pressure pushes the winds outward in all directions. My machine releases electrical particles, which results in a lowering of the pressure. In other words, the configuration of the isobars is drastically altered by the ions in the air. Now do you understand?"

"Perfectly," muttered Einstein, pushing back his glasses.

"Do you really understand what Rayn said?" whispered Mrs. Anderson.

"Yes," answered Einstein. "What he really said is that he wants to collect a lot of money from the people of Sparta."

"But what about his machine?" Mrs. Anderson asked.

"I don't think there is any machine, and if there is, it certainly wouldn't work."

*Can you solve the mystery:* How did Einstein know that the machine wouldn't work?

"How can you tell that the hurricane machine doesn't work without even seeing it?" Mrs. Anderson asked during a brief intermission.

"Because of something Rayn said," Einstein explained. "He said the winds around a hurricane are caused by its high pressure. That's exactly wrong. Air pressure drops quickly toward the center of a hurricane. In fact, a hurricane is a large area of *very low* pressure, not *high* pressure at all. The low pressure is what causes the great winds to blow inward toward the center of a hurricane."

"Then his machine can't work?"

"Not a hope," continued Einstein. "Rayn said that his hurricane stopper lowers the air pressure. If his machine did lower the pressure, it would make a hurricane even stronger. And all that business about ions and isobars was only to confuse people into thinking that his machine was really scientific."

"I guess Professor Rayn doesn't know much about hurricanes."

"Right," said Einstein. "In fact, he knows so little that if he said, 'Good evening,' I'd call the weather bureau to make sure."

# 4

## The Case of the

# FANTASTIC WATER POT

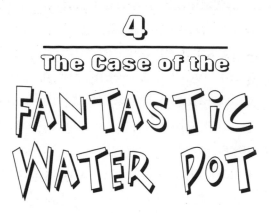 have an invention that will solve the energy crisis, Einstein," Stanley said. "I'll probably get a medal from the president and make a lot of money besides. People will be lining up in the stores to buy my incredible energy saver."

"Is your new invention like the windmill you designed?" Einstein asked. "You remember the fifteen-foot-tall windmill, don't you? You set it up on top of your mother's car so that it would turn while the car was moving and generate electricity. It worked fine until your mother drove under a bridge that had a thirteen-foot clearance. Say, did your mother ever replace the roof on her car?"

"That's a kind of painful subject, Einstein. I wish you wouldn't mention it anymore. Mom got so angry at me that she made me clean up my laboratory. It took me nearly three weeks."

"Your lab doesn't look any different to me," Einstein said. He looked around Stanley's "laboratory"—an attic room that Stanley's parents let him use for his experiments. The room was overflowing with all kinds of stuff. It looked like a junk shop. But Stanley claimed that it was filled with important scientific apparatus.

Stanley Roberts was a teenaged friend of Einstein's who was also very much interested in science. Stanley was in high school and Einstein was only in middle school. So Stanley often showed off his inventions to his younger friend to teach him how a "real" scientist worked. Einstein liked Stanley but enjoyed kidding him.

"I wish you'd stop getting me off the

subject, Einstein," Stanley said. "You won't believe the invention I'm going to show you. It really works. But what I'm going to show you has to be kept in strict secrecy. I don't want anyone stealing my ideas."

"Oh, you can speak just like a hot dog to me," Einstein said.

"What do you mean, like a hot dog?" Stanley asked with a puzzled look.

"You know—frankly," said Einstein.

"You know the whole world is facing an energy crisis," Stanley said, ignoring Einstein's joke. "Well, I've invented a pot that boils water much faster and uses much less heat than a normal pot."

"And that's going to solve the energy crisis?" Einstein asked.

"Maybe not solve it, but it will certainly help. Can you imagine? People will be able to cook food much more quickly and therefore more cheaply."

"That certainly sounds good," Einstein admitted. "I'd like to see your invention work."

"Here it is," Stanley said proudly. He

lifted a sheet that had been covering his lab table. On the table was a pot on top of a double electric hot plate.

Attached to the pot was a glass funnel and a hose. The hose was connected at the other end to a machine under the table.

"What's that?" asked Einstein, pointing to the machine on the floor.

"All in good time, Einstein," Stanley said. "First let me tell you how I got the idea. I was reading a book about mountain climbing. In the book the author mentioned that water boils very quickly on high mountains because the air pressure is so low. And then the idea came to me in a flash. Suppose I hook up a vacuum pump to a pot. The vacuum pump will pump air out and lower the pressure in the pot, and the water will boil much more quickly. That will save a lot of energy."

"But, Stanley," Einstein said, "don't you know that—"

"Let me prove to you that it works," Stanley said impatiently.

He placed another pot alongside the first one on the hot plate.

"I'm going to fill both pots with exactly the same amount of water," he said. "One of the pots is hooked up to the vacuum pump and the other isn't. Both pots will be heated the same. Let's see which one boils first."

Stanley flipped on the switches under the double hot plate. Then he flipped the switch on the vacuum pump. In a short time the water in the pot with the hose attached was boiling rapidly, while the water in the open pot was just beginning to steam.

"See?" Stanley said proudly. "My fantastic water pot really works. It's going to make me rich and famous. What do you think now, Einstein?"

"I think you'd better not start spending any of your millions before you get them," said Einstein. "I'm afraid that even though the water boils sooner in your fantastic water pot, it won't cook foods any faster."

*Can you solve the mystery:* Why won't Stanley's "fantastic pot" cook foods faster than an ordinary pot?

"I don't understand why you say that, Einstein," Stanley said. "You see that the water is boiling much faster in my fantastic pot. Won't that cook foods much more quickly?"

"I'm afraid not," Einstein said. "It's true that water boils more quickly when the air pressure is lower, but that doesn't cook foods any more quickly. In fact, it is exactly the reverse. On top of a high mountain you can't even cook a hard-boiled egg in a pot of boiling water."

"What are you talking about, Einstein?" Stanley asked.

"Water boils at a much lower temperature when the air pressure is very low," explained Einstein. "On top of a high mountain water boils at ten or fifteen degrees lower than at sea level. But the boiling water is not very hot, and foods cook very slowly at the lower temperature."

"I see what you mean," Stanley said thoughtfully. "I guess my fantastic pot won't make me a millionaire, after all."

"Don't be sad," Einstein said. "A millionaire just sits all day on top of gold, while just think who sits all day on *silver.*"

"Who sits on silver?"

"The Lone Ranger, of course," said Einstein.

# 5

## The Case of the

# iMPOSSiBLE BEND

"C hildren," Ms. Taylor said, "the school fair is scheduled for next Friday. There will be a used-book sale, a cookie and cake sale, and the usual kinds of booth activities, such as bobbing for apples. All the money earned from the fair will be used to help pay expenses for our school's long weekend at Big Lake State Park later this month."

Ms. Taylor paused as the class started to buzz. Everyone was looking forward to the fair and also to the weekend at Big Lake. Ms.

Taylor, Einstein's sixth-grade science teacher, waited a few minutes and then called on the class to quiet down.

"I want to appoint a committee to decide on our class booth at this year's fair. Try to come up with something different. The class that earns the most money with its booth will go up to Big Lake a day early. Now who would like to serve on the committee? Hands, please."

Many children raised their hands to volunteer. Ms. Taylor chose six children, including Pat Burns and his pal Herman. She chose neither Einstein nor Margaret.

Later, during lunch recess, Margaret was talking to Einstein. "I wonder why Ms. Taylor didn't choose either of us for that committee," she said. "Does she really expect Pat the Brat or Herman to come up with an original idea?"

"Well, it's only fair that everyone gets a chance," Einstein replied. "And maybe Ms. Taylor thinks that scientists can't come up with a contest that's fun."

"I guess that's so," Margaret said glumly.

"You haven't even cracked one joke all day long. Maybe too much science makes you lose your sense of humor."

"Lose my sense of humor!" exclaimed Einstein. "Not very likely! I'm just like the scientist who invented spaghetti. I can use my noodle to come up with an idea for a booth that will be the hit of the fair."

"Look, noodle head," Margaret said sweetly, "talk is cheap. Let's see you come up with a *science* booth that is funny and attractive. The committee is supposed to report tomorrow on their idea for a booth. Why don't you come up with your own idea? If it's better than the committee's idea, I'm sure the class will go along with it."

"I accept your challenge," said Einstein. "Science *can* be fun. In the meantime, let's go and eat an astronaut's favorite meal. Launch."

The next day the committee was giving their ideas about a booth for their class. They had elected Pat the Brat chairman because he had volunteered for it. Pat said that he would make a good chairman. Besides, he pointed out, looking at his fist, he was also the strongest kid in the class. No one else on the committee was prepared to argue the point.

"Here's what we decided to do," Pat reported to the class. "We're going to have a fortune-telling booth. I'm going to dress up with a turban, and we'll get a crystal ball. Then we'll charge ten cents apiece to tell people's fortunes."

35

"But, Pat, what do you know about telling fortunes?" Ms. Taylor asked.

"I could make them up," said Pat. "Who's going to know the difference?"

"Sure," called out Einstein, "Pat could dress up like a lady, and we could call him Miss Fortune."

Pat glared at Einstein. "O.K., wise guy," he said. "You got a better idea for a booth?"

"It just so happens I have," answered Einstein. "Suppose our class has the Booth of the Impossible Trick. You have to pay a dime to try it out, and if you can do the trick, you win a dollar."

"But who's going to try to do an impossible trick?" asked Pat.

"That's the good part," said Einstein. "The trick sounds like it's easy to do, but it's really impossible. We should gets lots of people who'll try to win."

"That's stupid," said Pat. "How can a trick sound easy if it's really impossible?"

"Do you want to try it?" asked Einstein.

"Do I have to pay you a dime to try?" Pat asked suspiciously.

"No, this is for free," said Einstein. "All you have to do is bend over and touch your toes without bending your knees."

"What?" said Pat. "That's easy. I'll bet you a dime I can do that."

"There's just one more thing, Pat," Einstein said. "You have to begin with your back and your feet touching a wall. Your feet have to remain against the wall as you bend."

"So what?" said Pat. "I'm strong. I can touch my toes anywhere."

"Sorry," said Einstein, "but it can't be done."

*Can you solve the mystery:* How does Einstein know that Pat cannot touch his toes without bending his knees when his feet are against a wall?

Pat stood up against the front wall of the classroom and laughed. "Can you imagine?" he said. "Einstein is telling me that I can't touch my toes. Maybe he thinks I'm as weak as he is."

Pat started to bend over, but he quickly lost his balance. "Let me try that again," he said. Again Pat bent over and nearly fell down. He tried to do it several more times and then said in disgust, "That's impossible. No one can do it."

"That's just what I told you, Pat," said Einstein. "The trick sounds easy, but it's really impossible."

"Einstein, that's really a great idea," Ms. Taylor said. "I think it will make a terrific booth at the fair. Everyone will want to try it out. We can put the tryout place behind a curtain so that no one can see it's impossible to do."

Margaret raised her hand. "I agree with you, Ms. Taylor," she said. "It really is a great idea. Science *can* be fun. But why is the trick impossible? Can you explain it to us?"

"Certainly, Margaret," replied Ms. Taylor. "The trick is impossible because...er...Would you please explain the trick, Einstein?"

"Sure," said Einstein. "It's all a matter of your center of gravity. That's the point where all your weight is concentrated. If your center of gravity is directly over your feet, then you're O.K. But if your center of gravity moves to a point outside your feet, then you fall over."

"But then how can you touch your toes at other times?" asked Ms. Taylor.

"Well, when you bend over freely, you shift your upper body weight forward and move your lower body weight backward at the same time. That keeps your center of gravity from moving outside your feet. But with a wall at your back, you can't shift your lower body weight backward. All your weight moves forward. So you fall over when you try to touch your toes."

"That's wonderful, Einstein," Margaret said to him later. "I'm sorry I called you a noodle head yesterday."

"It did me some good," said Einstein. "As Frankenstein said when he was hit by a bolt of lightning, 'Thanks, I needed that.'"

"You certainly haven't lost your sense of humor," Margaret said. "Unfortunately!"

# 6

## The Case of the

# DISTANT STARS

onight is the big event," said Einstein. "I've finished my telescope's tripod, and we can go out in the backyard and do some stargazing."

"It's about time," said Dennis. "You've been working on that thing for months now. And you said the telescope was ready to use weeks ago. Why couldn't we look at the stars just by holding the telescope in our hands?"

"It wouldn't work," Einstein explained. "An astronomical telescope is too powerful to be hand-held. You'd never be able to keep it steady enough to observe anything."

"Then how come sailors are always looking through telescopes that they hold?" Dennis asked.

"That's not the same thing," said Einstein. "A ship's telescope may have a magnification of ten or fifteen. But even a small astronomy scope will magnify forty or fifty times. And the higher the magnification, the steadier the mounting you need. Wait till it gets dark—you'll see why the tripod is so important."

That night the boys ate dinner quickly and did the dishes in record time. It was dark by the time they carried the telescope and its mounting out to the backyard.

"That doesn't look much like a telescope to me," Dennis said after Einstein had set up everything. "Where's the glass lens at the front?"

"This is a reflecting telescope, not a refractor," Einstein said. "Refractors gather light by means of a glass lens at the front end of a tube. That's the kind of scope that most people recognize. But a reflector gathers light by means of a curved mirror at the bottom of a tube. A reflector is easier to build and much less expensive for the same size."

"Whatever you say, Einstein," said Dennis. "Let's look at some stars,"

"Before we look," said Einstein, "let's wait a few minutes for our eyes to become dark-adjusted. Close your eyes for a little while. After your eyes adjust to the dark, don't look directly at my flashlight. If you look at a bright light, you'll lose your dark adaptation quickly."

"O.K.," said Dennis. He closed his eyes. "Are you thinking of becoming an astronomer?" he asked.

"I might," Einstein said. "Of course you know that an astronomer is a night watchman with a college education," he continued.

"Ha, ha," said Dennis, opening his eyes. "Could we look at some stars now?"

"Sure," said Einstein. He set up the telescope on the heavy tripod and pointed it at a spot in the Milky Way. Then he motioned Dennis to look through the eyepiece.

43

"Wow!" Dennis exclaimed. "I see so many stars I can't even count them. What am I looking at?"

"That's a small section of the Milky Way," said Einstein. "It's a huge mass of millions and millions of stars. They're so far away that without a telescope they just look like a band of hazy light. The Milky Way is a group of stars called a galaxy. Our sun is part of the Milky Way, out toward one edge. You're looking toward the center of the galaxy."

"Let's look at that bright star next," Dennis said, pointing.

"That's not a star, it's a planet," said Einstein.

"How can you tell without even looking through a telescope?" asked Dennis. "I thought planets move around in the sky so that they're in different spots all the time."

"That's true," Einstein admitted. "I'm not sure which planet it is, but I do know it's a planet."

*Can you solve the mystery:* How can Einstein tell a planet from a star without using a telescope?

"It looks like a star to me," said Dennis.

"There's a difference," Einstein explained. "Except when they are high overhead, stars twinkle when you stare at them. Planets usually shine with a steady light."

"Why is that?" asked Dennis.

"Stars are so far away from us that they look like points of light even through the biggest telescopes. Planets are much closer than stars. A bright planet will look like a disk even through my little telescope. We get many light rays from a planet but only one ray from a star. The Earth's atmosphere can interfere with a star's light much more easily than with a planet's light. When it does, the stars appear to be twinkling."

Einstein looked through his telescope at the planet. "I think the planet is Jupiter," he said. "The four faint points of light you can see nearby are Jupiter's moons. Just think. The moons were first seen by the great scientist Galileo with a small telescope more than three hundred years ago."

Einstein paused and smiled. "You know that some people say Galileo would have

been a great movie fan because he liked to
watch the stars so much."

"Ugh!" said Dennis. "I think you should
stick to being a night watchman."

# 7

## The Case of the

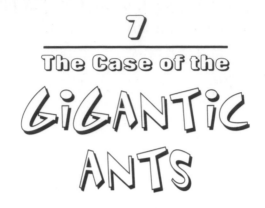

# GiGANTiC ANTS

his is more than just a pet, Einstein," Stanley said. His long black hair fell over his eyes, and he impatiently pushed it back. "I think this animal may be a perfect solution to the energy shortage."

"Let me guess what kind of pet you're sending for this time," Einstein said. "It's a flame-throwing dragon with wings. During the summer the dragon will go around lighting people's charcoal barbecues. During the winter the dragon will light the wood in fireplaces."

"That's the silliest thing I ever heard of," Stanley said, shaking his head.

"I guess it is," Einstein agreed with a smile. "Almost as silly as your sending for the green monster last fall."

"Don't remind me, Einstein." Stanley shuddered. "What a mistake I nearly made. It's a good thing I realized what it was in time."

"*You* realized!??" exclaimed Einstein. "That's not exactly how I remember it!"

"Well, I really don't recall all the details," Stanley said with a wave of his hand. "Anyway, let's forget that. See if you can guess what kind of animal I'm sending for now. I'll give you some clues."

"Before I guess that, maybe you can guess what to do with a green monster?"

"Einstein!!!"

"Wait till he ripens," Einstein said hurriedly.

"Why does a smart kid like you make jokes

like that?" asked Stanley with a groan.

"Because they're *wise*cracks," Einstein quickly explained.

"I'll forget you said that," Stanley said. "All right, here are some clues to the animal I'm going to send for. This animal can carry many times its own weight. It can climb straight up a wall. It can fall from a tall building and not get hurt. What is the name of the animal?"

"It sounds like a superanimal, leaping over tall buildings at a single bound," Einstein said.

"Well, I guess you might call it a super-animal," Stanley said. "I'm talking about an ant."

"You know, you're right," Einstein said. "I didn't think of ants or other insects. They can do all those things you said. I remember watching an ant carry a twig that was twice its size."

"You see?" Stanley said. "This time I came up with something that will work. We can use ants to carry things, and that will help create a new energy source."

"What!?" Einstein exclaimed. "You mean you're going to train millions of ants to get together and carry heavy objects?"

"Don't be silly," Stanley said. "I'm not going to use tiny ants. I'm going to use gigantic ants the size of people. I saw an advertisement in the back of a magazine for gigantic ants. This person spent many years breeding ants to become very large. Now he's offering them for sale."

"You mean he's going to ride one over to your house?" asked Einstein.

"No, wise guy," Stanley said. "He sends them out in the mail just after they've hatched from eggs, when they're still pretty small. I'll keep them in the garage, and then when they're full-grown, I can ride them or hitch them to a wagon to carry things. Can you imagine! A person-sized ant will be ten times stronger than the strongest horse!"

"I'm afraid not." Einstein sighed and shook his head. "It will never work."

*Can you solve the mystery:* Why can't Stanley use gigantic ants to carry things and help solve the energy shortage?

"Just tell me why not."

"Because a person-sized ant is impossible," said Einstein.

"How do you know?" asked Stanley.

"An insect is strong because it weighs so little," Einstein explained. "Let's say that an ant could become one thousand times bigger. Its weight would go up one thousand times its length, multiplied by one thousand times its height, multiplied by one thousand times its width. That's one thousand times one thousand times one thousand."

"But wouldn't its strength go up the same amount?" asked Stanley.

"No," said Einstein. "Its strength would only go up by the cross-sectional area of its muscles. That is, the increase in muscle fiber, or width times height. That would be just one thousand multiplied by one thousand. So a poor gigantic ant's weight would go up one thousand times more than its strength."

"That means it wouldn't be able to carry anything," said a disappointed Stanley.

"It wouldn't even be able to carry itself," Einstein said. "A gigantic ant would collapse under its own weight. Gigantic insects are just for science-fiction stories—they can't really exist."

"Well, as a matter of fact, the advertisement I saw was in a science-fiction magazine," Stanley said sadly.

"By the way, there is one kind of gigantic ant," said Einstein.

"Really? Which ant is that?" Stanley asked.

"An eleph*ant*," answered Einstein.

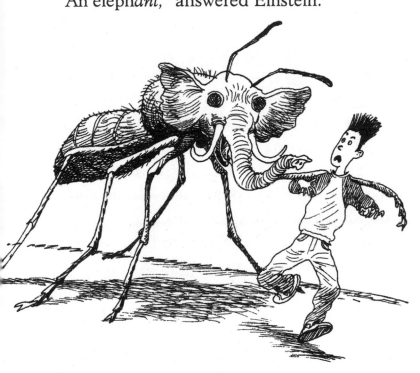

## 8

# The Case of the

It looked just like an African plain. Zebras, giraffes, and antelopes were grazing on the grass in small groups. A pride of lions—one large male, several females and their young cubs—lazed about in the shade of a clump of trees.

"Can anyone tell why the lions do not try to catch the other animals?" Ms. Taylor asked her sixth-grade class at the zoo one morning.

"Maybe they're not hungry," Herman said.

"That's stupid, Herman," Pat said. "Lions are always hungry. There's a big ditch between the lions and the other animals. That's why they don't eat them."

"That's right, Pat," said Ms. Taylor. "But how did you know? You can't see the ditch from here."

"I'm just smart," Pat said.

"Yeah, he is," Herman said. "Besides, Pat visited the zoo two weeks ago with his family. Right, Pat?"

"Who asked you, Herman?" Pat exclaimed.

"I'm sorry, Pat. Did I say something wrong? Aren't you smart? What did I say?"

"Nothing, Herman. It's quite all right," Ms. Taylor said. "Now I want everyone to listen carefully. I know you'd all like some free time to look around the zoo with your friends. So I'm going to give you a free hour before lunch. I want all of you back here by twelve noon. Any questions? See you all in an hour. Don't get lost."

"Let's get out of here quick before Pat and Herman decide to tag along," Einstein whispered to Margaret. "I had enough of them on the bus coming down here. All they're interested in doing is playing tricks on other kids."

"I couldn't agree with you more," Margaret said. "If Pat had tried to grab my lunch box one more time on the bus, I was going to bop him on the nose."

The class quickly scattered in all directions. Einstein and Margaret decided to walk over to the large-mammal house. It usually contained elephants, rhinos, hippos, camels, and giraffes. But during hot weather the animals were kept in large open pits connected to their inside cages.

Please do not feed the animals. Please do not throw anything into the cage.

Each pit had a sign with the name of the animal and some information about it. There were also signs that read: PLEASE DO NOT FEED THE ANIMALS and PLEASE DO NOT THROW ANYTHING INTO THE CAGE.

Einstein and Margaret looked at the elephants first. Without reading the sign, Einstein pointed out that they were Asian elephants.

"How can you tell?" Margaret asked.

"Asian or Indian elephants have smaller

ears than African elephants," Einstein explained. "Also they have a slightly humped back. African elephants are a little sway-backed."

Einstein paused. Then: "Say, Margaret, you know the best way to catch an elephant?"

"How?" Margaret asked.

"Act like a nut and he'll follow you anywhere," said Einstein.

"So start acting," Margaret said with a laugh. "Let's walk around and look at the giraffes. They're one of my favorite animals."

Einstein and Margaret had just turned the corner of the large-mammal house when they saw Pat and Herman. Pat was leaning over the ledge surrounding the giraffe pit. He seemed to be trying to reach something with a long stick.

"What are you doing, Pat?" Einstein asked. "Are you trying to bother that giraffe?"

"We're not doing nothing wrong," Pat said. "I'm just trying to get the ball out of the giraffe's cage. We were just coming around the corner when we heard the giraffe scream. Some kids were teasing the giraffe. They

threw the ball at it. Herman and me ran over
and chased the kids away. Now I'm just trying
to get the ball back."

"You're not telling the truth, Pat," Einstein
said.

"How do you know?" Pat said. "You didn't
see me throw the ball."

*Can you solve the mystery:* How does Einstein
know that Pat is not telling the truth?

"I know you just made up the story about those kids, because you said you heard the giraffe scream," Einstein said. "But a giraffe can't scream. Most of the time it makes no sounds at all, and even the loudest sound it makes is a sort of low moan."

"O.K., Einstein," said Pat. "But we really weren't trying to hurt the giraffe. We just wanted to wake him up. So we tossed the rubber ball at him."

"But suppose the giraffe ate the ball and it got stuck in its throat?" Einstein said. "It might have choked to death. It was stupid of you to throw the ball. You better get one of the zoo-keepers to get the ball before anything happens."

After Pat and Herman had gone to get a keeper, Margaret said to Einstein, "You know they should have read the sign about the giraffe. It explains that a giraffe doesn't have vocal cords and can't 'speak.'"

Einstein smiled. "Does the sign also explain how a giraffe makes the most of its food?"

"What do you mean?" asked Margaret.

"He makes a little go such a long way," Einstein said.

# 9

# The Case of the

# LOST

# HiKERS

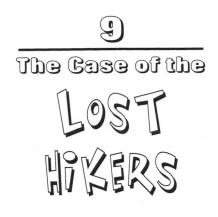

t was Sparta Middle School's annual weekend trip to Big Lake State Park. Einstein's sixth-grade class had just arrived, a day earlier than the rest of the school. That was their reward for earning the most money at the last school fair.

In the morning the boys and girls swam and played ball. After lunch they had free time until five in the afternoon. Einstein, Margaret, and their friends Sally and Mike decided to explore the shores of Big Lake.

Along the way Einstein spotted a large

bird making lazy circles in the blue sky. He pointed out that its broad wings and short fan-shaped tail meant that it was a hawk. Through his binoculars Einstein could see that it was a red-tailed hawk.

"Let's go in the direction the hawk is flying," Einstein said. "Maybe we can find where it nests."

"What kind of nest does it make?" asked Mike.

"They usually build a nest of sticks high up in a tree or on a ledge," Einstein answered.

"But we don't want to bother the hawk," Margaret said.

"We won't," Einstein said. "If we can find where it nests, we'll just watch through binoculars."

"I thought hawks killed chickens," said Sally as they started to climb.

"Not often," Margaret said. "Mostly they eat mice, rats, and other rodents. Hawks used to have a bad reputation. But now most people know that they do far more good than harm."

After a while the trail in the woods vanished and the going got much rougher. The boys and girls had to scramble over branches and fallen trees. The hawk appeared and disappeared from their view. Einstein and Sally had scratches from thorny bushes and low-lying branches.

"I'm getting tired," Sally said. "Let's sit down and rest."

"Yeah, then I think we should start back," Mike said. "We're having a big campfire tonight, and we're supposed to help prepare the food. I'd like to go for a swim before it gets dark."

"Good idea," Margaret said. "Let's start back. That hawk's nest may be miles from here."

"I think you're right," Einstein said. "I'm getting tired of watching that hawk like a hawk."

Everybody groaned in response to Einstein's joke. After a few minutes of resting, Margaret stood up and looked around. "Which way is back?" she asked.

"I think it's that way," Mike said, pointing in one direction.

"No, I think it's that way," Sally said, pointing in a different direction."

They all stood up and looked around uneasily. They could see only a short distance through the dense woods in any direction. There were no trails and no markings.

"Let's just go," said Mike.

"But which way?" asked Margaret. "If we set off in the wrong direction, we'll only get more lost. We can even wander around in circles without knowing it. Does anyone have a compass? I know we were traveling to the north. All we have to do is to keep going south to get back to the lake."

"But which way is south?" asked Sally. "Nobody has a compass."

"If we wait until night, we can tell by the stars," Mike said. "We can use the polestar to locate north."

"I don't think we should wait till night," Einstein said. "We might get separated in the dark, and nobody even has a flashlight."

"But we've got to do something," Margaret said. "You got us here, Einstein. What should we do?"

"What kind of watch do you have, Margaret?" asked Einstein. "With hands or with numbers?"

"What difference does that make?" Margaret asked impatiently. "My watch has hands and the time is four o'clock."

"I don't want your watch to tell me the time," Einstein said. "I want it to tell me how to get out of here."

*Can you solve the mystery:* How can Margaret's watch help Einstein find the way back?

65

"Here's my watch," Margaret said. "Let's see you do your thing."

Einstein took the watch and held it flat. He looked up and turned the watch so that the hour hand pointed in the direction of the sun. He pushed back his glasses and thought for a minute. "That direction is south," he said, pointing. "Let's go."

It was ten minutes to five when the small group returned to their campsite on Big Lake. "Just time enough for a swim," Mike said as they scattered to get their swimsuits.

"Hold on," Margaret said to Einstein.

"Explain how the watch told you the direction."

"Sure," Einstein said. "You know that the sun is due south at noon. Suppose we point the hour hand at the sun at that time. Then both the hand and the number twelve will point south. Before noon, the sun is left of the number twelve, and after noon the sun is to the right."

"But the sun goes around once in twenty-four hours, and the hour hand of a clock goes around twice," Margaret said.

"Right," agreed Einstein. "So you have to halve the angle between the hour hand pointed at the sun and the number twelve. Here's how it works. You point the hour hand at the sun. South lies midway between the hour hand and the number twelve."

"Amazing," said Margaret. "I never realized that a watch could tell you direction."

"Not only that," Einstein said, "if your watch is broken, you can't even go swimming."

"Why not?" asked Margaret.

"Because you don't have the time," Einstein said, walking away rapidly.

# 10
## The Case of the

# CROWDED DOCK

t was Saturday, and the other classes were arriving on school buses at Big Lake State Park. Einstein's class was on hand to greet them.

"It's such a shame you had to go to school yesterday," Pat called out to the new arrivals. "You should have been here. We went swimming, played ball, and had a great campfire at night. I thought of you while we were toasting marshmallows. Too bad my class had the greatest booth at the fair. But we always beat the rest of the school."

"I don't think Pat should keep rubbing it in that way," one of Einstein's classmates said. "They're liable to get mad. And there are some seventh and eighth graders who would be only too happy to pick on our class."

"I agree with you," Margaret said. "I don't know why Pat is boasting, anyway. It was Einstein who thought up the idea for the Booth of the Impossible Trick."

"Pat sure does think a lot of himself," Einstein said. "On his last birthday he sent his parents a telegram of congratulations."

Pat turned and glared at Einstein. "I heard that crack," he said, "and it's not funny."

"Neither are you, Pat," said an eighth-grade boy who was just getting off the bus. "In fact, I'd make myself disappear if I were you. Understand?"

Pat looked as if he were about to answer, but then he motioned to Herman and they walked away.

"It's a good thing Pat walked away," Margaret said. "For a second I thought he was going to start a fight with that eighth grader. That would have been a mistake. That kid is much bigger than Pat."

"It would have been a world's record," Einstein said. "The first time Pat ever had a fight with someone bigger than himself."

"Let's forget about Pat," Margaret said. "Why don't we go fishing off the dock? Maybe we can catch some fish for supper."

"Good idea," said Einstein. "Let's dig up some worms for bait and then get hooks and lines."

Half an hour later Einstein, Margaret, and a few of their classmates were happily fishing off one side of the dock. Children from other classes filled up most of the spaces along the other sides. There wasn't much empty room left when Pat and Herman strolled up.

"You kids move over and make some room for me and my pal," said Pat to a group of fifth graders.

The younger children moved over, and Pat and Herman sat down. Pat took out some fishing line and tied one end to a hook. He measured out a long length and tried to break the line. But it wouldn't break.

"Well, look at that," said an eighth-grade boy sitting nearby. "Strong man Pat kicks away the fifth graders but then can't even break a piece of fishing line!"

"Yeah," agreed his friend. "Those sixth-grade kids are just a bunch of bigmouths."

"Is that so?" Pat said. "You guys are just bigmouths yourselves. We can do anything you can do. You can't break this fishing line with your bare hands either."

"Maybe we can and maybe we can't. Would you like to make a bet on it? The kid's class that loses has to move off the dock."

"It's a bet," Pat said. "Your strongest kid against our strongest kid. I'll be back in a minute."

Pat ran over to where Einstein was sitting. He explained what had happened and said, "Einstein, you got to come up with some science that will help us win. Otherwise we're going to have to get off the dock."

"I don't know why you get us into these things, Pat," Einstein said. "But that's an easy bet to win. I should be able to break your fishing line with my bare hands without too much difficulty."

"I hope you're right," said Pat. "That eighth grader looks like he's twice your size."

"Don't worry," Einstein said. "Unless he knows how to hold the line, he'll never be able to break it."

*Can you solve the mystery:* How does Einstein
plan to break the fishing line?

73

The eighth graders came over and gathered around the group of sixth graders. The biggest one took the fishing line and held it out to Pat.

"Not me," said Pat. "Einstein is going to break the line."

"O.K., Einstein," said the eighth grader. "But remember. You have to break the line using only your bare hands."

"Sure," Einstein said, pushing back his glasses. "Why don't we both try it at the same time? The first one to break the line wins."

The eighth grader cut off two equal-sized pieces of fishing line and gave one to Einstein. "Ready, set, go," he said. He tugged at the line with both hands and nothing happened. The line was too strong. It only cut into his skin.

Einstein took his piece of line and wrapped it around his hand in a curious way. Then he pulled, and the line broke with a snap. The sixth graders cheered.

"I guess the sixth grade wins," Einstein said. "But let's just forget about the bet.

74

There's enough room on the dock for all of us."

After the eighth graders had moved away, Einstein explained to Pat and his other classmates how he had broken the line.

"The important thing," he said, "is to loop the line against itself. That concentrates all your force on the tiny spot where the line crosses. The line itself acts like a knife blade. When you suddenly jerk your hands apart, the line cuts through itself."

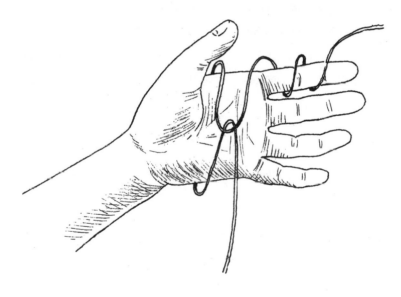

Einstein showed them how to loop the line around one hand. Then he wrapped the line several times around his other hand, a foot below. He closed his hands into fists, brought them close together, and then suddenly pulled them apart. The cord snapped at the point the line was looped.

"I'm glad I could help you out this time, Pat. But remember, everything has its breaking point," Einstein said, "including people."

"Not me," said Pat, walking away.

Einstein turned to Margaret. "The trouble with Pat," he said, "is that whenever he stops to think, he forgets to start again."